MANIMUKTO

SRIMAT SWAMI DEV PRAKASH ARANYA

ISBN 979-888569127-7

Contents

Foreword *v*

Preface *ix*

Acknowledgements *xi*

1. Chapter 1 1

Foreword

There is a saying in English that "Well begin is half done" which means that if you start a work in your mind, that work is half done. I have been thinking for a long time that I will write a book. It's been a long time since I've been able to find a place to live, and it's been a long time coming, and I'm glad I did. But book's and soil never betray you. "That is, everything in life can deceive but spiritual books, books of gods, biographies of great men and soil do not deceive anyone. Then I started reading the scriptures and whatever I read made my heart feel or feel. That is what I am writing in this book. Why did I give the name of this book Manimukto? The words of the great men came out of their mouths like pearls like pearls.

I am not a writer. I don't have the knowledge to write a book. I never had any desire to write a book. I am very incompetent in language and caste knowledge. I pay my respects to my Supreme Guru Sri Sri Samadhi Prakash Aranya Maharaj, the Supreme Personality of Godhead, whose great power has made my desire to write a book strong. Introduction is needed first to write any content. I do not have the knowledge or power other than the full Brahmaguru, his resources or grace. I am a child of a very low level from the land where it is possible to write a role if you get the mood. So when I went to write the introduction, I remembered the prayer of the famous poet Michael Madhusudan Dutt.

No, I am the poet Guru Bhava Padambuje Balmiki, O Shirasurashcha Moni of India, then the follower slave Rajendra Sangam Deen, as far as the distant pilgrimage is concerned, only you are the source of your grace. My

Gurudev's Absolute Gurudev Srimat Swami Hariharananda Maharaj's book Patanjali Yogadarshan which is a Calcutta University textbook, has recorded some of his quotes from it. My Gurudev's guru brother Srimat Dharmamegh Swamiji which has been published from Madhupur Kapil Math under the name of Shantilipi Granth. I read that textbook and recorded in my heart what came to my mind. Not without mentioning the name of the person who has always inspired me to write this book and why I have named this book Manimukta. His name is Smt. Sona Ghosh, daughter of Amar Ghosh, a resident of Hasua Math. She is a teacher. Astrologer and writer Shiva Shankar Bharati. He has come in contact with many great men. I have found so much wonder and inspiration in reading his written travels and books of saints from the first to the third volume, which I have repeatedly read the first volume and memorized and memorized. I have traveled from Jalpaiguri to Calcutta three times to meet him. I'm unlucky, I don't know his address, I haven't seen him. Later I got the address from Sea Brothers Padmapratim Roy Chowdhury in Kolkata and Narkeldanga 55/5 6th Floor Road Kolkata 11. I went to his house to meet him. I went at seven in the morning and saw a lot of crowd. Everyone has come to see the wrestling hand. It is written there that those who are impatient will not sit here, they will have to wait. The name is written at eight o'clock and he comes to the chamber at eleven o'clock. I sit and wait for four hours. I am already talking to an old woman. Knowing that I had come from Jalpaiguri, he gently leaned on the stick and approached her, telling her about me. Anyway he comes to the chamber at 10-30 o'clock to see me. After everyone ate Humri. I stand silently and do not get a chance to speak. Then I say a word in English, "I have some imminate talk with you.

He looked at me and motioned for me to enter the chamber. I talk to him a lot and I ask him again and again and ask permission to write that invaluable message of travel and sainthood in my Manimukta text. He did not allow. Then I gossip about what is written on a piece of paper. How can people find happiness and peace in the world? He stared at my face for a long time and remained silent. Then I realized that silence is a sign of consent. In any case, if the meaning of this book is accepted by the devotees and dear readers, then I will consider myself blessed.

I have tried with caution. I apologize for any inconvenience this may have caused, but I am sorry for any inconvenience.

Humble -
Dev Prakash Aranya Maharaj

Preface

OM TAT SAT

AOHAN

"Gurudev Gurudev Gurudev,
Gurudev eso he, eso he, boso he, boso he
Amar o hridoy asone.
Ami dhoyaibo, tobo ratul choron, Noyon solilo sinchone
Gurudev eso he, eso he, boso he boso he,
Amaro hridoy asone.
Dhup dip mala rekhechi sajiye
Tomari ashay rekhechi bosiye
Tumi je Moder praner debota
Tai cheye achi ami path pane
Gurudev eso he, eso he, boso he, boso he,
Amar hridoy asone.
Samadhi santane dake onukkhone
Onjoli dite tobo Shri chorone
Bodon o voriya pronob jopibo
Tomare rakhiya samne
Gurudev eso he, eso, he boso he, boso he,
Amar hridoy asone."

Acknowledgements

Gurupranam

He Gurudev ami tomay kori pronam
Benche thakte kore jabo tomar gungan
Tomar Ashish peye, ghurechi e vubane
Dekhechi e prithibike tomar sannidhane
He Gurudev ami tomar kori pronam
Benche thakte kore jabo tomar gungan.
Tumi amay shikhiyecho, vokti kare bole
Doya-dan-dhormo-adi koto ki shekhale
He Gurudev ami tomay kori pronam
Benche thakte kore jabo tomar gungan.
Tumi shudhu pashe thako pujibo tomar chobi
Tomar ashirbad pele, peye jabo sobi.
He Gurudev ami tomay kori pronam
Benche thakte kore jabo tomar gungan.

CHAPTER ONE

At the Brahma moment (at three o'clock in the night): You have to wake up in the morning, come in the morning, wash your hands and feet well, sit in bed and chant for one hour and meditate for one hour.

Then the palms of the hands should be matched towards the front and the pearls should be seen in the hands. Moni - Another name for pearls is Ratnakar. Ratnakar Akar, Ratnakar is the name of the sea. Then it should be said - "Pratahsmaranam"

1) *Pratah ruthay sahayat sahayat prat runtat yat,*
karemi jagat matah stutadeva tab pujanamah.

(If he recites these two lines of mantra, his day will be very good.)

2) *Bramha muraranta puranta kari 'vanu' 'shashi' vumi suta budhashcha*
Gurushcha, shukra shani rahu ketu kurbenta sabe sama-suprabhatam.

(If he recites these two lines of mantra, all his planetary idols remain calm.)

3) *Lokesh Chaitanya Mayadhideva Srikantu Vishnu.*

Bhavadajnyayeb, pratah samurthayatab priyathang sansara jatra manuvarttashishe.

(Reading these two lines of mantra does not cause any disease in his body.)

4) *Punah shlok nala raja chah*
Punah shlok Yudhishthir
Punah shlok Chang Vedehi
Punah shlok janapurna.
(There is no shortage of meaning when reciting these two lines of mantra.)

5) *Ahlya Draupadi, Kunti, Tanra Mandodari Tatha,*
Panchakannya Swarantat Mahapatak Nashanam.
(If you recite these two line mantras, there will be no quarrel, quarrel, unrest with anyone.)

Then while breathing in the left nostril, Basumati should be bowed with her left foot on the ground. Then apply basil on the floor with soil. Once the soil is dry, take a good bath before sunrise. (There is no pain in the body when rubbed on the ground of Tulsi floor.) After bathing, whether it is a boy or a girl, while chanting Guru Mantra, water should be poured well on the head. If the Guru Mantra is not taken, then he has to take a bath facing north while naming a deity and at the same time he has to say, "Om Gangge Chong Jamuna Chong Godavari Saraswati, Narmada Kaberi Sindhuh Jal Humne Sannidhat Kurung. Om kurukshetra gaya ganga prabhas puskara nichah tirthane tani punyani snanan kale bharbasthiti." (You have to take a bath by saying this mantra three times.)

Bathing very early in the morning reveals twelve times in the body—

1) The ghost does not fall into the eyes of the demon.
2) Tamasic feeling goes away.
3) The mind is full of joy and strength grows in the body.
4) There is no disorder in the body, that is, the body is healthy.
5) Increases holiness in the body.
6) Increases body brightness. That is, there is beauty and the softness and elegance of the body increases.
7) The voice is sweet, the fragrance is increased, the pronunciation is beautiful and innocent.
8) Everyone has respect, devotion and respect.
9) Everything is accomplished, mental spirits increase.
10) There is wisdom in the path of religion.
11) Everyone adopts him.
12) Can adapt to any place.

This time after bathing, 'Om Sri Vishnu' remembers this name three times, prostrates, and first he will rub his chest. Then wipe the head and body. Never wash your hands, feet or feet with a dry towel. Then the towel will match the shade. Never let the towel dry in the sun. One thing everyone says here is that if you take a bath in the morning, or in the morning, it will get cold, and it will get very cold. Nature or God has created some qualities in the body to protect this body from cold and heat. Which is our ignorance or we do not know how to protect the body from cold or hot hands. Now coming to the word of that rule—

Time is given in the calendar, the sun rises and sets every

day When the sun rises we breathe in our right nostril and breathe out in our left nostril. It lasts for an hour, changing every 1 hour. This goes on all day long, again when the sun goes down, inhale in the left nostril and exhale in the right nostril. It lasts for an hour and changes every 1 hour. In this way, 21,620 breaths continue throughout the day and night, and what does the body do?

There are 72,000 nerves in our body (including veins and sub-veins) in these 21,620 breaths. It intercourse with 72,000 nerves and kills all the nerves (killing them) by blowing and hitting only three women. Awakens. (The sound of a hammer blowing with a bronze bell) Breath-breathing All the nerves (dying) The breath that fills the stomach with air and exhales to the left is called laxative, meaning carbon dioxide, and if it is held in the body without exhaling, it is called kumbhak. By this supplement, laxative and potter, when Ganga-Jamuna-Saraswati (Ira, Pingala, Sushma) is awakened, the pranayama of the body begins (i.e., to stop the movement of one's wind by sacrificing life air.)

Then the divine vision of man is opened, that is, the trinity of man is awakened. (Like the three eyes of Durga, the three eyes of Mother Kali, the three eyes of Shiva) Then man has foresight and can say man's ghost, future, present and by leaving this body man can go from one planet to another, then come back to the body.

Anyway, let's see how the cold and hot breath that is drawn to the right side of the body is called Surya Nari. The breath that is drawn on the left side is called Chandra Nari.

It can be done - if the sun pulse is closed with cotton for one hour then the body gets cold and if lunar pulse is closed with cotton for one hour then the body gets hot. If you practice breathing in this way, the body can be cooled and heated. If you close the left nostril before taking a bath in the morning, your body will be warm and you will not feel cold. On a hot day, if the sun veins of the right nostril are closed by cotton, the body will get cold. By practicing continuously in this way, after one year, the sun pulse and the lunar pulse stop and start on their own, that is, the body can be cooled and heated.

After bathing every day, take a bath whenever you can. You will bow—

Suryadhyana

'Om'
Om Raktamba Jasan Mashesh Gunaik Sinduh
Vanu Samasta Jagata Madipang Bhajami
Padmadaya Vyaar Ban Dadhitang Karaijya Manikong
Mouli Marunang Ruching Trinetratam

Suryapujamantra

Om Bhagavate Sri Surya Namah

BeejMantra and HingMantra

Mulamantra— *Om Hring Hong Song or, Om Ghrining Surya Adityang*

SuryaDanMantra

Om Namah Bbisbate Brahmanang Bhasbate Vishnung Tre Drushe Jagat Savitre
Shuchaye Savitre Karmadayine Idmayang, Om Sri Surya Namah

SuryaPranamMantra

Om Jaba Kusumang Shankasang Kashyapayong Mahadutim Dhannatvaring
Sarvapapoghna Pranotahasmi Divakaran.

Now after bowing to the sun, take 1 jug of water, clean the basil floor well and pour another jug of water on the head of the basil tree. He has to say that -

'Tulsi Tulsi Narayana
Tumi Tulsi Brindavan
Tomar Shire Dhali Jal
Ontim Kale Dio Sthal.'
Or, Om Govinda Vallabhang Devi Bhakta
Chaitanya Karinim
Snapayami Jagat Dvatring
Vishnu Bhakti Pradayinim.

Leaf picking mantra

You have to clap your hands three times and say that—
Dale Krishna patay Hari

Sare baso Krishna tuli.

The mantra of giving light

Mothers and sisters should say with the hem of the sari on the head—
Tulsi talay dilam bati
Sakshi thako Ma Bhagawati,
Sakshi thako jato Devgan
Sakshi thako Narayana.

Tulsi Pranam Mantra

Om Vrindaye Tulsi Divya Piyai Ke Shabasyach Vishnu
Bhakti Prade Daivisatah Bait Namah Namah

It is a good thing that everyone has a basil tree in their house Tulsi trees and the soil under the Tulsi floor have special significance. Not only in the name of Narayan but also for the health of everyone in the house, the Tulsi tree and the Tulsi floor should be taken care of, water should be given and lamps and incense should be burnt on the Tulsi floor every evening. Resulting in health and peace.

Tulsi Pradakshina Mantra

Namah Namah Tulsi Krishna Beloved, Radha - Krishna's service will be given to this aspirant. Whoever remembers you, his desires are fulfilled. Please do it, Vrindavan people, Namah Namah Tulsi Krishna Beloved, Radha - this aspirant will get Krishna's service. Tulsi, take this offer. Sakhi's permission to do the service with the right to be a slave. This desire in the mind, live in luxury kunje, harib sada in the eyes, twin ruprashi namah namah tulsi krishna preyasi, radha-krishna's service will get this desire.

Dino krishna dase kaya ehi yaan mor ho sriradha govinda gune premanande bhasi— Namah Namah Tulsi Krishna Beloved, Radha - Krishna's service will be given to this aspirant.

Quality of Tulsi leaves: According to Ayurveda, Tulsi tree cures various ailments. The basil plant works well in the treatment of heart disease and ischemia. Dr. P.G. has done research for five years. There is no rule to stop the consumption of ugly, basil leaves, when you can chew as many raw leaves as you want.

Tulsi leaves have been recognized as the best among the medicinal herbs This tree has been given the highest place in Matria Medica.

Application of Tulsi in daily life:

1) Chewing two or three Tulsi leaves on an empty stomach every morning in the month of Kartik will not cause any disease in the body throughout the year. The application of basil leaves in the weather in the month of Kartik always keeps the body healthy.

2) Basil leaves naturally bring selfishness and concentration of the heart, if someone is angry for any reason. Then if you just put on clean clothes and hug the Tulsi tree and put soil (a small amount) on the floor of the tree or roll it on the floor of Tulsi, the anger immediately calms down like water. Sitting or standing near a basil tree increases mental concentration.

3) Adding basil leaves to food or food during solar eclipse

or lunar eclipse does not affect the effect of polluted weather during eclipse.
4) Basil tree is said to be a symbol of spiritual peace. Lighting a lamp on the floor of Tulsi and walking around the Tulsi tree brings wonderful peace of mind.
5) The smell of basil destroys blood disorders.
6) Before bathing, if you take a bath with some basil leaves in water for a while, you will not get any skin disease.
7) Drinking that water with basil leaves in a pot of drinking water will not cause any stomach related disease.
8) The body is always energetic and healthy if you hold the Tulsi garland in your voice.
9) Tulsi controls libido. Increased libido in its natural or limited form.
10) Chewing basil leaves does not cause tooth decay, the teeth are strong and bright. Increases the lifespan of teeth.
11) Massage with basil leaf juice strengthens bones, relieves fatigue, keeps the body healthy. Applying basil juice instead of soap, oil, cream etc. gives various physical benefits.
12) If someone suffers from epilepsy, then before taking a bath on Saturday and Tuesday morning, hold your breath and lift the black basil tree in one go and hold it with the black car thread in your right hand. (If it is hysteria but it will not be good.) After bathing will hold, there are no other rules.

Now let's talk about eating, before eating something yourself, you have to take 1 glass of water (3 glasses) on an empty stomach. After 10 minutes before eating anything yourself—

1) The birds need to be fed. (Business is good in this.)
2) You have to feed the cow before eating anything by

yourself. (It increases prosperity and keeps the planet calm.)

3) Dogs need to be fed before eating anything by themselves. (In this, the enemy also becomes dear, brother. The enemy has to be given a big seat. The enemy does not have to criticize, the enemy has to be loved, the smile has to be conquered with affection-sweet words.)

4) Before eating something by oneself, the ants have to be fed. (There is no need to lend a hand to anyone, there will be no debt.)

5) You have to feed the fish before eating anything yourself. (It brings back lost property.)

It is absolutely impossible for worldly people. If you want to eat fish, you have to give up eating fish (meat) and be a prasad bhoji. Then the daily routine will do whatever it takes.

Remember: When eating, always remember your Gurudev or Ishta Devta and put the rice in your mouth first. Then when you go out, remember the name of the god Ishta and Gurudev, you will go to any work. Before going to bed at night, remember your favorite deity and go to bed remembering Gurudev. Remember, never lie down with your head facing north. It is scientifically unhealthy. After bathing, Gayatri will recite mantras in her mind while looking at the sun.

Gayatri mantra.

'Om bhuh bhubasvah, tats sa bittu barenyam,
bhargadevasya dhimahi dheyang yong nong prachyadayat om.'

After chanting this mantra three times with reverence and devotion, he becomes a Brahmin and his mind is full of joy and happiness.

The meaning of Gayatri mantra is: To look at the sun and say, O Merciful One, purify my heart. Cleanse me, lead me from darkness to light. Free yourself from the influence of the vocal senses.
Always keep away from sinful deeds. Your grace is the source of my life. Lead me to the path of peace and liberation.

Om shanti, Om Shanti, Om Shanti.

Mahamrityunjaya Mantra:

Om Triyambakang Yathamahe Sugandhipushti Vardhanam, Ubaruk Mibbandhanath Mrityur Mukshiyo Mamritata.

(If you chant this mantra three times with reverence and devotion, there will be no disorder in his body. The disease which is supposed to last for seven days will be gone from two days.)

Then the daily routine will do whatever it takes and remember to do it by hand while working. Suppose the house is being swept or the house is being wiped, then the work will be done by hand, the name will be on the face Someone is talking or you are talking to someone.

If you want to perform puja after bathing, you have to sit facing north or east with your own seating in clean clothes. If there is an idol or a photo of a planet or a deity or a guru, you have to stand in front of it three times and say 'om, tat sat'. If someone or people are in front, there is no need to listen. Then you just have to put your hand on the earlobe and say 'Om tat sat'. If you say this three times, all the faults and errors in that work will be refuted. Then you have to put your hand on your chest and say, Thakur, forgive me my wrongs - crimes, faults, errors. Then you have to kneel down and say, Thakur, forgive me all my wrongs, crimes, faults and mistakes. Then you have to bow your head on the ground and say, Thakur, forgive me my wrongs - crimes, faults, errors.

Asana Shuddhi Mantra: If you want to purify Asana, you have to hold the Asana on your head and say, O Asana, you are for the sake of Brahma, don't leave me till you get Sriguru Padpadma, Asana. You have to hold the chest and say the same thing. The same thing should be said with the head on the seat while keeping the seat on the ground.

Then you have to sit on the seat and remember the devotional goddess and say, O devotional goddess you are also for the sake of Brahma. Don't leave me until you get Sriguru Padpadma. You have to say that three times with folded hands.

Mukhsuddhi mantra: If you want to do mukhsuddhi, take water in the palm of your hand (Ganga water is better). Ganga remembers Goddess - *Om Namah Sri Vishnu, Om Namah Sri Vishnu, Om Namah Sri Vishnu,* the words must be said.

Bhoot Shuddhi Mantra (Deh Shuddhi): If you want to purify the body, you have to say— '*Om Apabitra Pabitrava Sarba Obasthaya Yata Hapiba Ya Amare PundariKaksha Sa Bajjhantara Shunchi, Om Shunchi, Om Shunchi*' Then you have to sprinkle water on your body.

Bathing Mantra: Water should be said on the palm of the hand, *Om Gange Chah Yamuna Chah Godavari, Saraswati, Narmada, Kaberi Sindhu Jal Hashmine Sannidhang, Kurung Om Kurukshetra GayaGanga Pravas O Pushkara Nichah Tirthane Tani Punnani Snan Kale Vabashthiti.*

Now you have to sit well in the seat and fold your hands and say— *Om Pabitrata, Om Pabitrata, Om Pabitrata, Om Pabitrata, Om Pabitrata* (Five times in total) This has to be said. O merciful Lord of all worlds, Brahmastra, keep me free from all sins and make me worthy of your grace. Lord, I am a sinner, by your grace I am liberated, I am remembering you with all my heart. Correct me 9. Guide them also into the good behaviors and to avoid displaying some profane ones. Give me strength to do my duty in life. May I always remember you.

Then take a look at the photo or the idol and keep your eyes on the power —

'Om Namah Paramatmane Namah
Om Namah Paramatmane Namah.' (2 times)
The union of Paramatma with
Atma is Brahma, Sohom Om.
Paramatma is the absolute relative. Absolute Gurudev.

Keep an eye on the photo or the idol (eye to eye power) take energy from it. Then you have to chant. (1 hour is better.) After chanting Vishnu mantra or meditate on Vishnu.

Vishnu's meditation:

'Om dhey sada sa bittu mandal madhyabartti narayana sar sijasan san sannavisthang keurban konak kundalban kiriti hari.

Hiranmaya pudhurta shankha chakra. Om Namah Brahmano Debayo Go Brahma Brahmano Hitaya Chah, Jagaddhitaya Krishnayo Govindayah Namah Namah.

Puja's Mantra:

Om Namah Vishnobe Namah.

The Mul Mantra:

Om Namah Narayan Namah.

Vij Mantra:

'Om'

Home mantra:

Om tadvabishnu parama padang sada paryanta surayeh devir choksura tatang.

Mantra of giving Tulsi to Vishnu:

Om Namaste Bahu Rupaya Vishnabe Paramatmane Swaha.

Then the one who will do the deeds and will chant the Guru Mantra in his mind while doing the deeds. While chanting any food, one should sit on the seat, sprinkle water on

the food place, keep the food purse in hand, take water in hand and turn the hand three times and say— *'Om Bramhar panag Brahma Hari Brahmasna Hutam, Brahmei Batenag Gantabang Brahmakarma Samadhina— 'Hari Om Tat Sat'*
Or, *Om Sahanababatu, Sahanaubhunattu, Sahabrijang Karbabhai - Taijasbina bardhitamastu ma vidisabhai 'Hari om tat sat'.*

Eating any food facing east increases life expectancy. Playing facing west brings financial prosperity. Playing facing south, the name is Yash. Moti is played on the path of religion by facing north. Taking food on wet feet increases life expectancy. Wet feet will catch the disease.

You can rest at noon, roll, but not sleep. In the evening, wash your hands and feet well and chant after wearing clean clothes. Never eat or move your face very early in the morning or in the evening. At this time the demon Pichasara eats, at this time the game is followed by the sight of food. In their eyes the body after the outbreak of the disease from contaminated food. When sleeping at night, wash your hands and feet well, put on clean clothes, face north and east of the bed and sit as a babu and chant. At the end of the chant, the feet should match the front and look at the big toe. Gently grasp the two thumbs with both hands and then, gently straighten and release the body towards the back.

On the left side of the pillow, tap the Guru Mantra or the name of the deity you like by tapping the ring finger three times in the pillow and say in your mind that - 'Every day every way I am getting better and better.' (you have to say 21 times) then you will see very good sleep. Never lie back on the right side due to a mistake. Return to the left side then return to the right side. If you sleep with your head facing east, you will sleep better. Sleeping with your head facing west will cost more than your income. If the music is more than the rent, that is, if it is 400 rupees, it will cost 1200 rupees. If you sleep with your head facing south, the deity will dream and will sleep well. When you sleep with your head facing north, you become unconscious, there is no stability. The mind becomes divert. Which one to leave and which one to do (there is no direction). In this case, do not sleep with your head facing north. The scriptures say that Ganesha's head was cut off in the north. Remember to never lie down with your head facing north.

It's scientifically unhealthy, we should wake up and first open our hands and look at the nose with our hands before getting out of bed. The side where the air is falling through the hole, the foot should be thrown on the ground first and the bed should be left.

'OM'

The utterance of *om* and the greatness of *om-kar*: Remember the sound of *om-kar* is an absolutely powerful and powerful sound. This onkar sound must be done before uttering any mantra. Because, at the beginning of the mantra, all the faults of the *om-kar om* mantra are destroyed.

Om = a, u, m, = a + u + m This is described. A = Brahma, U = Vishnu, M = Maheshwar. Therefore, the word Brahma, Vishnu, Maheshwara refers to Parabrahma.

***'Om Tat Sat'* - these three words are the name of Absolute Brahman. Brahman, Veda, Yajna - these three combine**

to create. Therefore, the Brahmanists, by uttering the word 'om', perform the rituals of austerities, sacrifices and almsgiving as usual. 'Om Tat Sat' will always pray, *"O God, I want you, see that your world does not fascinate me with the splendor of Maya, I want you."*

This time I am coming, how can people get happiness and peace while living in the world. I will come later in the words of happiness. What is happiness? And how to get it? I am talking about how to get peace.

Our Acharya Param Gurudev Late Sri Sri Mad Swami Hariharananda Maharaj, Madhupur Kapil Math (Bihar) near his ashram Deoghar is now Jharkhand. While he was still alive, two of his favorite disciples were alive, but now they are gone.
1) Our Gurudev Late Sri Sri Swami Samadhi Prakash Aranya Maharaj;
2) Late Sri Srimad Swami Dharma Megh Prakash Aranya Maharaj.

Acharya Srimamat Swami Dharma Megh Swamiji had transcribed the utterances of Acharya Param Gurudev, which is now published from Madhupur as Shantilipi Dharmagranth. On the first page of that peace script there is a letter called Patnika, in which it is written and in the chapters of the peace script there is a series of how people can find peace in the world. In the prayer Gitanjali of our Samadhi Math, that Patnika is written. What is written? I am transcribing it from there - 'Affordability is better than happiness in words. We all want relief or peace, peace is the desire to suppress the restlessness of the mind, what a beautiful thing - comfort or peace. Which we all want.

Where is the relief or peace? It is available in our hands without asking. What kind? The deer does not know that it has deer lotus in its navel, it is beautiful, fragrant, it runs dry like crazy. We are the jewels of Ratnakar Ratan.

Ratnakar is the name of the sea. (Gemstone diamond jewelry is found at the bottom of the sea.) We need to wake up the gemstone that is inside us. That means we have to wake up from within with relief or peace. What kind? In Srimat Bhagavat Gita, Chapter 10, Bibhuti Yoga, verse 26, is given. That is, among all the trees I am Ashvath, among the Devarshis I am Narada.

Among the Gandharvas I am Chitrarath and Siddha, among the great men I am Kapilmuni:
1) If you want to live in the world, that is, if you want to get peace, you have to live like a banyan tree. Just as crows, eagles, vultures, etc. live in a banyan tree, so in this body - lust, anger, greed, addiction, alcohol, nesting like a bird. In the month of Fagun Chaitra, the kind of leaves that actually fall off, the devotee calls it sadhana or the worldly people or the devotees call it sadhana, that is, by chanting or by knowledge, they will keep all of them asleep or numb. If you are a little careless again, those ripu will be awake.

2) Just like a traveler takes shelter under a banyan tree, to survive the sun, storm, water, rain, winter and summer, to live in such a world, to get peace, one has to be happy with the happiness of others and sad with the sorrow of others. After taking shelter, the passer-by makes the place dirty, that is, leaves the cooking excrement, etc., and nothing comes of the banyan tree. In this world or in this world, whatever you do, you will never find his mind. He will hurt

you or try to harm you.

3) Shepherd boys or small children play and break the branches of the bot tree. Pull out the glue. Similarly, if any of your relatives or acquaintances ask you for anything or money, if you have it, give it to them immediately. Remember, mistakes don't hurt and you don't want them back. If not, you will speak with a smile and affection, no, brother, I don't have it, now I can't give it. If you ask for money or things back, you will become his enemy. He may not say anything but in his mind he will insult you or think you are an enemy. You will think that not even two days have passed. In this way, if the world is like a banyan tree, it seems that at least some military peace can be found.
Now let's come to the second word, if there is no desire and no anger, the agitation of the mind is dispelled. Happiness is followed by fulfillment of desires. So we want happiness, so peace is our ultimate goal, what is the way to that peace? The work of the third chapter of Srimat Bhagavata Gita is given in verse 36.

Arjuna ubaca:

Athah Ken Prayukta Hayang papacharitang purushang anichchinapi, vasneya baldib niyajitang

That is, man driven by someone according to his will - if he does not want to commit sins or commit sins.

In reply, Lord Krishna said to Arjuna in verse 37—

Shri Bhagwan Ubach

Kam M Krodh S Rajgun Yamudbhav
Mahashana Mahapapna Ma Biddha Naimih Vaibinim,

That is to say, Lord Krishna told Arjuna that this lustful anger arising from Rajaguna can never be quenched by Mahabhakshaka i.e. Bhoga. And you will know that the one who commits the most sins is the greatest enemy.

In the same way that ghee is offered in a fire, the fire burns with a blaze of fire, so the desire is increased by the desire and it is stopped by the sacrifice. So what is the need for lust, anger, greed, delusion, addiction? It also needs - what kind? Work, work is also needed. His wish is for that conch, chakra, mace, lotus, Narayana or Vishnu, so that I may be on the right path, walk honestly.

Anger: Anger is also needed. On top of that I would get angry or angry that my mother would slander, father would slander and guru would slander. I will protest if I have the strength, otherwise I will leave the place. Because, Gurudev's slander, mother's slander and father's slander are not heard.
Greed: I will desire to gain him, that is, I will try to gain Ishtadev and Gurudev in my heart all the time in my dreams.

Addiction: I have to give up my thoughts, I have to think of everyone, everyone is mine.

Wine: I will be fascinated to see Gurudev or Thakur Devta.

Matsarya: The word means grass-like sunichen: tarupi sahisnu: na amanibe manden, krtaniya sada hari, that is to say, to live in the world, must be dead than grass, tolerant like taru, manis must be obeyed and always praise God, good words Sadhana - to chant.

What is the way to peace? These way is to become aware of the two kinds of—
External civility i.e. yam, rules, kindness and charity and stability of heart, respect, anger, country. If there is desire, thirst, greed, violence, anger, etc., peace can never be found.
Therefore, the civilized ones, if they get rid of all the faults of the heart, then there is peace in them. Here it is said that one should be polite, steady, humble, polite, courteous on the outside and walk honestly on the same path with smiling and affectionate face in the same manner. Only then will civility come.

Desire: Looking at something or someone over and over again leads to addiction. Out of that addiction, the desire comes only when you desire to get that thing.

Thirst: Thirst is the desire to get that thing as soon as one is thirsty. If you are thirsty for this, after half an hour or an hour, if you drink a little water, the thirst is quenched.

Greed: The Scriptures say that the desire that is felt in the heart to get or eat something is greed. Increases greed for salt, for which it is forbidden to eat raw salt without cooking.

Violence: Violence is not just animal violence or animal violence, it is the act of inflicting physical or mental torture on someone and inflicting emotional trauma on the heart. It must be abandoned.

Anger: Anger is the name given to being unnecessarily aroused unnecessarily. Anger arises in the body to eat more salty, sharp objects, spicy (onion-garlic). Always stay calm. If you get angry, it will not work. For this, one has to be polite and chase away the guilt of the heart. Always be patient, steadfast, slow, steady, humble, polite, polite. But peace will be found.

Says again - there is no peace just by being civilized. Think donation is a civility, one can donate everything in one day. What to do then? If you want to donate then you want to get it again. In that you have to do evil to yourself. Peace can be found only by practicing the elimination of anger and hatred by protecting one's birth civility. What a beautiful thing. Here it is said that giving is a kindness. Why are we coming to this beautiful world? As a result of the blessings of the ancestors as a result of the good fortune of many previous births, I have traveled 84 lakh vaginas and got human birth, to pay off three debts.

1) Dev debt, 2) Sage debt, 3) Father debt

1) Dev debt: Donate with the right hand so that the left hand does not know. That is, there should be no feeling of arrogance. Pride is the root cause of human fall. What to do if you do not have the ability to donate? While the religion itself is moving, one has to recite Sad Granth, Dharmakatha,

Gita, Bhagavat. Even if you can't do it, if you have educational qualifications, then you have to give education to an orphan boy or a destitute boy or girl without any effort. If you can't do that, then do good to someone physically, that is, no one can pull a heavy bucket or anything with the weight of age, pull it or work hard for someone. If you can't do that too, then talking sweetly with affection is a debt.

2) Sage Debt: Atheists who do not consider God, God, God or Gurudev as their mother, are drawn to God by atheists, Ramayana, Mahabharata, Gita-Bhagavata, Chandi. Sage loan.

3) Father Debt: In order to increase the lineage, that is, in the act of filial piety, the wife is taken as a wife to produce a son. After having one or two children, husband and wife should be like brothers and sisters, like friends. In other words, husband and wife will be like Laxminarayan in the world. Husband and wife will respect Lakshmi with knowledge. The wife will worship the husband with Narayan knowledge.

The happiness of the family is due to the woman
The woman is beautiful due to devotion to Krishna.

It has been said again— that, in order to get rid of anger, one has to keep in mind the practice of sadhana. The great men who have pursued peace, first by maintaining civility, then by gaining heart, steadfastness, patience, form, mental strength, have aroused anger and hatred, and they are the ones who have given advice in pursuit of peace.

If you want to get rid of anger, you have to do japa, dhyana, sadhan-bhajan while sitting in the morning-evening seat at one time every day. If that is not possible then you have to name it in your mind (East name given by Guru). That is, do work in hand, name in mouth. Even if it is not possible, then one has to meditate on the East or meditate on the Guru's face and chant the name in one's mind every day. In that case, the mind will be polite. In case of anger or rage (excitement) one should immediately look at the big toe of one's feet and hold the big toe of both the hands in both hands and sit for a while and then the anger will subside and the mind will become calm like water. There is another way. If you get angry, if you roll on the floor of Tulsi and if you hug or walk around Tulsi Devi with the soil of Tulsitala in your mouth, then anger or rage will become as thin as water. Mental strength can be gained and peace of mind can be found.

Upanishad says that if there is Kama Yehasya Hudishrita in all the pramuchyas, that is, when all the desires of good and evil are sheltered in the heart, then peace is gained. Words of Acharya Param Gurudev (Sri Srimat Swami Hari Hara Nanda)

Puriyatbang Thinamasang
Priyong Kritvadvishampi
Pabang Gatba Sratoghyesya
Dhanya Banamupasate.

That is to say, by fulfilling the hopes of the earthly (before anyone asks for a thing or an object), he has to be loved by the enemies given to him, that is, he has to be loved by the enemies, he has to be given a big seat for sitting or he can be loved only by his obedience. By listening to the words of Dharma in the mouths of great men and by incorporating them in the heart, by gaining knowledge one can go after hearing or Moksha Vidya and all these pious people go to the forest and attain peace. If we want to have peace in the world, we must first make a resolution that (Tuesday, Thursday) can happen any day, Tuesday or Thursday is better because Tuesday is the birthday of our Guru. On that day Guru brothers and sisters worship Gurudev in every house again, Thursday Lakshmi or Lakshmi worship is done at home or, two days or four days may be Ekadashi, New Moon or full moon day, that I will be silent that day from sunrise to sunrise the next day (24 hours) I will fast or be silent, if that is not possible then from sunrise to sunset (12 hours) I will be silent.

Fasting does not mean fasting on an empty stomach. Here I am saying a word about fasting that if you worship by eating, you can get to God quickly. Revered Tagore Ramakrishnadev himself has shown Prince Siddhartha, on the other hand, learned Bodhisattva knowledge by eating sweets from the hands of Goalini named Sujata.

It is better not to eat only on the eleventh day. Because on the eleventh day all the sins of the whole world are present on the food. However, on any one day of the week or on the eleventh, the new moon or the full moon, I will not have a conversation or any discussion with anyone. I will remain silent.

Just in my mind, I will chant Guru Mantra or meditate or meditate, perform, bhajan of God. If I cannot remain silent, then I must resolve not to say more than necessary on that day. I will not criticize anyone unnecessarily. Sitting together or sitting with everyone will not laugh, joke, joke, nonsense.

I will not lie in the guise of mystery. I will not take any help from any order or servant etc. I will do my own work, I will not depend on anyone mentally. I will not gossip or chat, I will not be angry, I will not slander anyone, I will not criticize. Because we have to remember that this world is like a mirror and if there is any fault in the next one, he will suffer the consequences. But I am doing blasphemous deeds, I will have to suffer the consequences. All of this is given in the first chapter of the Peace Script. If you want to have peace in the world, you have to follow all these rules.

1) Every day in the morning from 4 to 5 in the morning to take a bath in the morning, even if you have a thousand jobs. It has to be done first. In it, the eyes of Alakshmi, evil spirits and demons will not fall on the body, even if it falls, it will be erased. Bad thoughts, bad dreams will be erased from the mind. No matter how much you are in need, even if you are worried about giving alms to the saints and beggars, it will be good for the family, if you do not get the saints, giving alms to the beggars will also work.

2) Don't say a word more than necessary. Mani must be respected. Before speaking, he will bite on the tongue, consider the place and time, look at the place-time-pot and speak sweetly with sweet words very affectionately.
Don't move your arms and legs, don't eat too much. Doing these, Alakshmi's vision falls. Lack in the world - Deficiency increases. No matter how bad the food is, whether it is good for the mouth or not, the food will be condemned from time to time. If you don't like it, don't eat, but don't condemn food, because mother Lakshmi's

position in food, if you condemn food, mother Lakshmi is condemned. It brings money and food trouble at some point in life. The body never stays healthy after eating the condemned food, after the outbreak of the disease in the world.

3)Those who want more life will eat any food facing east Name, if you want fame, you will eat facing south. Financially comfortable will face west for comfort. And those who follow the path of true religion and moral religion will eat facing north. If you can do this in the same way every day, you will see that the fruits will continue to grow from you.

4) Everyone in the family, Alakshmi lives somewhere in the house do you know? Bed in the house - Alakshmi lives where there is shadow in the bed and where there is darkness after lighting the lamp. So keep those two places clean and tidy every day. And, the place will be cleaned well every day and you will see that Alakshmi will not find a place in the house. The unrest will go away, the world will be blessed from the mind. Never eat anything in the early morning and in the evening. Don't move your face, the demon Pichasheras eat these two times, so when they play at that time, they catch sight of food. Diseases come from contaminated food in the eyes - the body, the peace of mind is lost.

5) Even if it is difficult, buy a little ghee. If there is a shortage, there is no need to buy more. If you can eat a little every day, it doesn't matter if you don't like it, while eating, you will sprinkle a little or a drop on others. Then eat one day or every day. If you eat like this, financial misery will be

cut off, prosperity will gradually come. I can't say whether I will be rich in it but money and food will be gone, there will never be a shortage in life. The words are unbelievable but true. If these deeds can be done by believing, then the results will be obtained. Even if disrespect can be done in disbelief and ungodliness, the result will be obtained. There is no fruit in this work. But if you leave it after two or ten days, nothing will happen. The work must be done in the future, if done with devotion, the result will surely match.

6) Do not sleep unnecessarily unnecessarily, it is called disease Do not draw on the ground with nails or anything. Peace of mind is lost and debt is incurred. People who have or have unseen eyes leave the grass with their fingernails, smile for no reason, eat large meals, get up in the morning, and sleep in the evening, write on the ground, play music on their body or seat. Never do these things, it will not benefit Lakshmi. Wash your feet thoroughly every day and keep them clean. Wet feet will take food will prolong life. But do not sleep on wet feet will catch the disease.

7) Listen, the wife of the house will not look at you when she is dressed or naked. In this the semen becomes turbulent, the vigor of the man is lost. One should not eat after one garment, the rule is to eat in one garment only during Shraddha of father and mother. Shraddha is eaten by playing after one garment. In this the body also becomes unhealthy in the world.

8) Many times you bathe naked in the enclosed place, undress your wife during Raman, never do it, it causes the sight of ghosts or evil spirits in the body. Over time the body becomes diseased, the mind becomes restless. Fire,

moon, sun, water, cows will never leave excrement in front of them. It destroys the intellect, one day or another will suffer from bladder related diseases. You will not think anything, nowadays since birth boys have been suffering from various diseases, no one is healthy. . Do you know why? After the sight of evil spirits or ghosts on the body of the wife during Raman being completely naked. None of you can see it. However, it is true that when a child is born, that effect remains. As a result, the body-mind-education of the child suffers from birth. That's why most of the children in the house are not human nowadays, nothing is beautiful or healthy for them. Don't eat fruit that birds have eaten, food that has legs.

9) Do not eat the fruit that is eaten by birds, will give up food that is eaten by the feet. Fruits, flowers, etc., which are stuck in the feet in any way, will not be suffered by the gods, it will be detrimental to oneself and the world. There is no food left over from the leftovers, the food eaten at the hotel and along the lines. Once you know the truth, it quickly infects the sins of others. Never eat food that has been touched by a dog or dried by a cow.

10) If the body and mind want the spiritual life and the welfare of the world, then the food and water will never be taken in any shraddha house except the shraddha of the parents. Playing the invitation of Shraddha is a great misfortune. The deterioration of the religious life of the body is inevitable. Playing prasad is the overall welfare. Sacrifice offered to the dead person is called prasad prasad. In the food after the sight of the ghost to enjoy the ghost. Eating this food makes the body sick and destroys the purity of mind, leads to unrest. The pleasure of the wedding

ceremony is called cum bhog, never eat. It leads to lust and enjoyment of the mind.

11) Eating in the other room, sleeping in the other bed is not good. Even if he gets a chance, he will not rejoice with another's wife. Touching each other's bodies, sitting together and eating together, sitting a few people in one seat (excluding wooden seats), sitting very close to each other, sitting side by side and whispering in each other's ears - all these will be abandoned. Absolutely know that the sins of others are quickly transmitted to these works. It will be a little difficult to do all these things, but if you try, all these are possible Many people do not know all these things, even if they know, they do not comply. Great lack of patience. As a result, the worldly people are suffering in one way or another.

12) The full fruit of the previous birth is lost - if the dust of the broom, the air of the cooler and the water for washing the hair is applied to the body. The deity gets angry when he lifts or leaves the air, so whatever happens during the chanting, touching the right ear with the right hand removes all faults.

13) Do not name any child in the world or name anyone after the goddess. It is better to name the goddess. But it is better not to keep the worldly. Do you know why? What is the similarity of the name with the name? If you think the name of a person Lakshmi, for some reason the girl did something wrong or crime. It can only be done if there is in the world, in which someone using the name Lakshmi used abusive language or cursed. In doing so, he aimed at a human-like body, in fact, indirectly hitting the

name of Goddess Lakshmi with a word wave. Because, the word Brahma, the goddess becomes indirectly angry when people notice. This ruined the peace of the girl's family life. If we notice a little, it can be seen that not a single boy or girl named Devdevi is at peace in the life of the family. There is no objection to naming gods and goddesses, but it is better not to hurt the name, it is good. But there is no way to be in the world.

14) Many people have a habit of beating drums before doing any good deeds, they will never do that. The more you keep secret about good or good deeds, the sooner you will be fulfilled. Before the work was done, he said that if the work was not interrupted, there would be a delay. Again, many times that work becomes a pond.

15) Many people see the dream of the goddess, do not tell anyone the benefits of 1 dream is lost. Anyone who has a bad dream has to call everyone. The evil of nightmares is destroyed. And sadhana-bhajan is not about talking about life or miraculous philosophy or any divine feeling. Even the wife should not tell the husband, it is a waste of God's grace. When told, they all slowly shut down.

16) Do not eat any food sitting on the bed. It calls for disease. Leaving food on the seat or taking too much food on hand does not mean eating slowly, it makes Lakshmi restless. Husband and wife do not have to sit down and eat together, even if they are financially comfortable, there will be no peace in the whole life, no matter how much you enjoy it? Its thirst will never be quenched, desire will never be quenched. Lust is restrained in moderation. The source of peace of mind is moderation.

Don't hurt anyone. The world will always be in the habit of enduring humiliation. All these habits can be successful with a little effort. If you can do this yoga, you will get peace of mind.
In the path of iniquity, which in the first stage, wealth, name, fame, fame, and destiny are all filled, the world is filled, and one wins unjustly. But rest assured that these are absolutely military. There is no forgiveness from God. Suddenly disaster will come in his life, it will be eradicated. It's not going to happen otherwise. One thing to remember is that if you have the infinite mercy of God, then people can laugh and open their hearts. He can sleep peacefully and get this grace of his easily from the world, if he does not take refuge in the path of iniquity and wickedness.

A lot has been said about that. It's better to do it, not better to do it. The cause or explanation of almost no words can be found. Why would it be? How is it possible to eat rice every day with ghee as the deficiency gradually goes away? The reason why the mind does not want to accept these things is—

That there are many dabs in a dab tree. A child is sitting under a tree with his father. The child has never seen a dab. The first thing my father heard was that dab was a fruit that contained sugar and sweet water. The child will not believe this. He will think, how is it possible? But Dad knows this is true because he ate both water and shells. It was possible for the father to know. The father did not know how the shell and water were formed inside the coconut.

This is because the sages of ancient India are ganchi, they

planted coconuts, the tradition is coming out of the mouths of those who ate it. Tradition is the truth about honesty. If you don't play, you will know how the shell and the water are inside him. We are children, I do not know, you do not know how the shell and water is being created inside the coconut? There is no question of faith and disbelief. It is an eternal truth that there is coconut shell and water.

Every human being who has some or the other problem stays with them The only way to get rid of this problem is to solve it. The way to get rid of any problem is to think about the problem first, then you have to think, is there any real problem? If I fall, what is the idea of the problem? Imaginary, military or deadly? If there really is a problem, then you have to think deeply first. We have to find a way to get rid of him. It is better to find a solution, but there is no harm in not finding one. You just have to be more discriminating with the help you render toward other people. Then, it will be seen that the solution will be found gradually.

The problem will be solved in a few days. Imaginary problem, I didn't get into trouble, but I think I will get into trouble, all these things have to be blown out of my mind. You have to think that if there is a problem then it will be seen, otherwise the peace of mind will be lost. The problem should not be rushed, whether temporary, imaginary or serious. Problems can never be overcome in a hurry, nor can they be solved. You have to be a little patient. You just have to be more discriminating with the help you render toward other people. How do you know? Remember the idea or the like or the universal, at least the eternal idea or the like wandering in the universe. Two are coming to someone's head, four and innumerable are coming to someone's head. Therefore, the idea or idea that is not coming to your mind about problem solving, may come to the mind of others. So if we discuss or consult, it will be seen that the solution will be found. Those who have social or family problems will read any good book. Reading good books calms the restless mind. Or it would be better to listen to a good book with someone. The work must be done at the same time every day, without missing a single day. If you continue with this rule for some time, at first it will go away, unwanted restlessness of mind, mental state will come, then you will find the way to solve the problem.

People do not have to despair, then the death of human life in this world will come quickly. One thing you should know for sure is that there is an obstacle routine in the great age. In that routine, every person is experiencing temporary happiness or sorrow in family life, this is the rule. That is to say, the sages of ancient India. When bad times come or go, you have to think it's temporary, then everything will be fine again. Again, when the good times are over, you have to assume that it will also fall into trouble again after a while. The world has everything. If you take a look, you will see that in this cycle of the great age, the life of a very healthy person is undergoing a radical change. Again the decline from the high position continues.

You know what I think? Most people today have no real goal or purpose. It is the result of a conflict of life and livelihood. It is causing thousands of problems. The goal agreement is also for those who have a definite goal or purpose to respond to various problems and injuries. And the funny thing is, people don't know what they want. But running is like confusion.

I firmly believe, deeply, that if a person has a goal, purpose and strong mental strength, then success in the world will not be an inevitable obstacle or problem for him. Lack of self-confidence and mental state leads to untimely death of human mind. As a result, there is always a problem in everything. Then people move forward at every moment on the path of death in this worldly life. That's not what I'm talking about. No matter how dark the front is, no matter how many problems are plagued in life, no problem can stop people from keeping the goal unchanged, unshakable.

Printed by Libri Plureos GmbH in Hamburg,
Germany